Five Favourite Tales
by Tony Ross

I Want My Potty · Oscar Got the Blame · I'm Coming to Get You · I Want a Cat · Super Dooper Jezebel

GUILD PUBLISHING

LONDON · NEW YORK · SYDNEY · TORONTO

I Want My Potty

"Nappies are YUUECH!" said the little princess.
"There MUST be something better!"

"The potty's the place," said the queen.

At first the little princess thought the potty was worse.

"THE POTTY'S THE PLACE!" said the queen.

So . . . the little princess had to learn.

Sometimes the little princess was a long way from the potty when she needed it most.

Sometimes the little princess played tricks on the potty . . .

. . . and sometimes the potty played tricks on the little princess.

Soon the potty was fun

and the little princess loved it.

Everybody said the little princess was clever and
would grow up to be a wonderful queen.

"The potty's the place!" said the little princess
proudly.

One day the little princess was playing at the top of
the castle . . . when . . .

"I WANT MY POTTY!" she cried.

"She wants her potty," cried the maid.

"She wants her potty," cried the king.

"She wants her potty," cried the cook.

"She wants her potty," cried the gardener.

"She wants her potty," cried the general.

"I know where it is," cried the admiral.

So the potty was taken as quickly as possible

to the little princess . . . just

. . . a little too late.

Oscar
got the blame.

This is Oscar . . .

... and this is Oscar's friend, Billy.
Oscar's mum and dad think Oscar made Billy up.

Whenever Oscar talked about Billy, his mum and dad said, "Don't be silly."

But Oscar and Billy were the best of friends . . .

. . . day and night.

Sometimes, Oscar let Billy have some of his dinner . . .

. . . but then had to eat it all himself.

When Billy left little bits of mud around the house . . .

. . . Oscar got the blame.

When Billy dressed the dog in Dad's things . . .

. . . Oscar got the blame.

When Billy put frogs in Granny's slippers . . .

. . . Oscar got the blame.

When Billy made breakfast . . .

. . . Oscar got the blame.

When Billy washed the cat . . .

. . . Oscar got the blame.

And when Billy left the bathroom taps running . . .

. . . Oscar got the blame

. . . and was sent to bed without a story.

"It's not fair!" said Oscar.
"Nobody believes in my friend Billy."

"THEY NEVER DO!" said Billy.

SUPER
DOOPER
JEZEBEL

Jezebel was perfect in every way. She was so perfect,
she was called Super Dooper Jezebel.

When other children came out of school, they were
sometimes untidy,

but Jezebel was always super dooper neat.

Jezebel always kept her room tidy, and she always put her things back in their boxes . . .

and she cleaned up after the cat.

When she went out to play with her friends,

Jezebel always kept clean. (She still liked to have two baths every day).

She always wrote her "thank you" letters, in neat
writing, without being reminded,

and at school, she was best at everything.

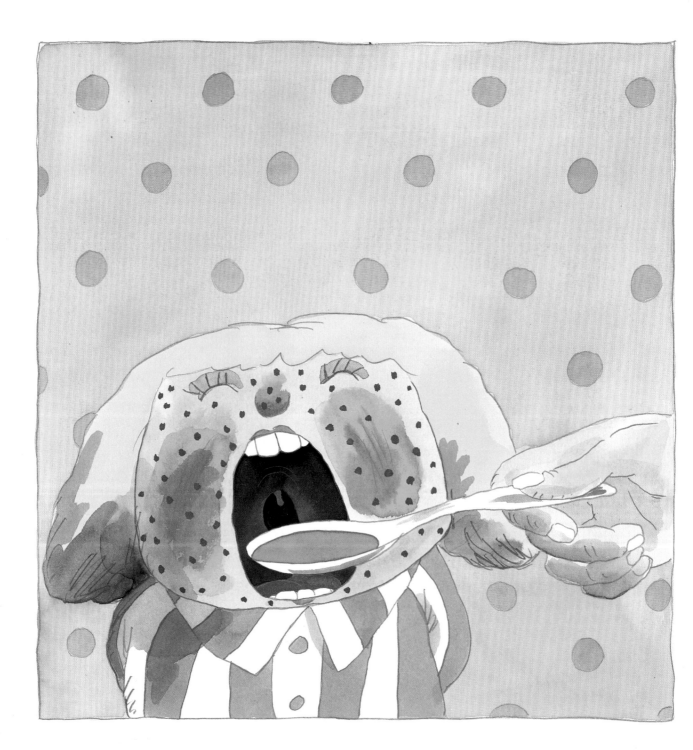

When she had spots, she always took her medicine
(and said, "Thank you.")

She could do up buttons, and tie real bows on her lace-ups.

Jezebel always ate up her meals. She always put her knife and fork together,

and she *never* picked her nose.

Jezebel told other children not to do things . . .

because it was nice being perfect.

When the Prime Minister heard about Jezebel,
she sent a special medal for being good,

and a special statue of Jezebel was put up in the park, to remind everybody else to try to be perfect.

She even went on television, in a special show
to talk about herself and her medal,

and the cups she had won for being polite, being
spotless, being helpful, being best at sums, reading,
poetry and writing.

At school, Super Dooper Jezebel wouldn't do *anything* wrong . . .

like the other noisy children who weren't perfect . . .

CLUMP!

I WANT A CAT

Jessy wanted a cat.

All her friends had pets.

Some of them had big pets and some of them
had little pets.
Jessy felt that she was the *only* girl in the world
with *no* pet...

And Jessy wanted a cat!

Her mum and dad always said, "NO!"
(Crawly, creepy, yowly things, they called them.)
So they kept giving Jessy toy cats instead.

But Jessy wanted a real cat.

Then…Jessy planned a wonderful plan.
She collected lots of fluffy white cloth, some
needles and cotton, and locked herself in
her room.

And she made herself a cat suit.

Next she took all of her proper clothes, and
buried them in the garden.
"I'm going to be the cat in this house," she
purred.

"What on earth do you think you're doing?"
said Mum.

"I'm going to be like this until I get a cat!" said
Jessy. "And if I *don't* get a cat, then I'm going to
be like this for *ever*!"

On Monday Jessy went to school.
When the teacher saw her cat suit, he shouted so
loudly, she jumped up on top of the blackboard,

and wouldn't come down, even for a saucer
of milk.

On Tuesday, Jessy went to a restaurant.
"Cats don't sit at tables," said Jessy. "Even in posh places."

"Milk and trout," she said to the waiter, "and please don't cook the trout. May it be served down here?"

"Certainly, madam," said the waiter.

Soon Jessy began to smell of fish.

When it was time for bath and bed, Dad went to
catch Jessy.
"Now you'll *have* to take that silly suit off," he
grinned.

"No I won't," said Jessy. "Not until I get a cat."

Then Jessy curled up on her bedroom floor.

In the middle of the night, Mum and Dad were roused by a horrible noise. It was like a million pigs falling downstairs, and the neighbours banging on the front door.

It was Jessy, on the garden wall.
"I WANT A CAT!" she was howling.

"Give her a cat," complained Mr Biggs from
next door.
"Give her a cat," complained Mr Figgs.
"Shouldn't be allowed," complained Mrs Figgs.
"Give her a cat," complained Mum.

So, early next morning, Dad went down to the
pet shop, and chose a cat. He took it to Jessy's
door, and knocked.

"Jessy," he called, "I've got a surprise for you."

"WOOF! WOOF!" said Jessy, "I WANT..."

I'm
Coming To Get You!

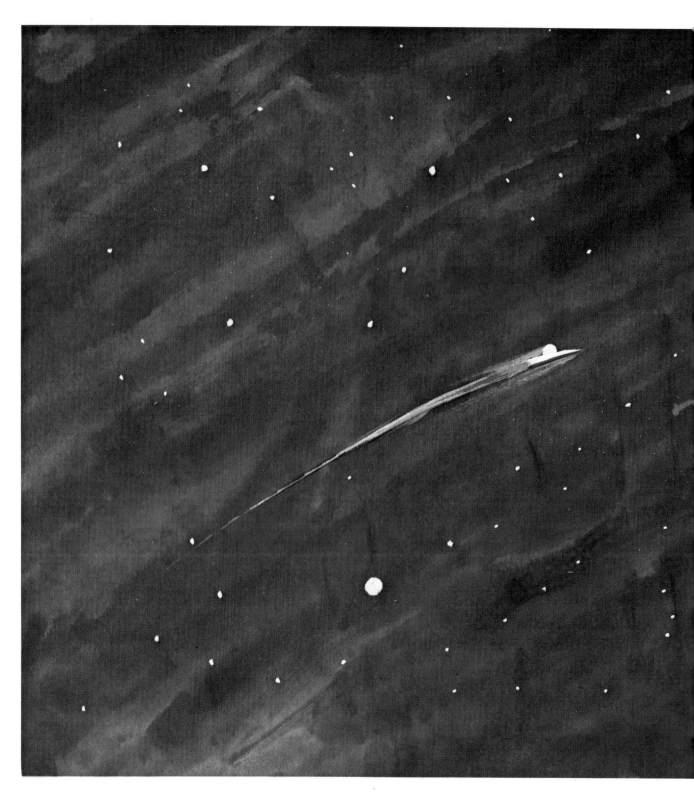

Deep in another galaxy, a spaceship rushed towards

a tiny, peaceful planet.

It landed, and out jumped a loathsome monster.

"I'm coming to get you!" it howled.

The monster crushed all the gentle banana people.

It smashed their statues, and scattered their books.

It chewed up the mountains,

and drank the oceans. It had the jellyfish for afters.

It gobbled up the whole planet, except for . . .

. . . the middle, which was too hot, and the ends, which were too cold.

Still hungry, the monster flew off in its spaceship, nibbling small stars on the way.

It had seen a pretty blue planet called Earth.

**The monster found little Tommy Brown on its radar.
"I'm coming to get you!" it roared.**

It was bedtime, and Tommy was listening to a story all about scary monsters.

The spaceship neared Earth, and the monster found out where Tommy lived.

It circled the town, looking for the right house.

As Tommy crept up to bed, he checked every stair for monsters.

He looked in every place they could hide.

Once, he thought he heard a bump outside his window.

**The monster hid behind a rock, and waited for the dawn.
"I'm coming to get you!" it hissed.**

In the daylight, Tommy forgot all about monsters, and he set off happily for school . . .

. . . but then, with a terrible roar, the monster pounced.